# The Three-Cornered Hat

in Full Score

## Manuel de Falla

DOVER PUBLICATIONS, INC.
Mineola, New York

*Bibliographical Note*

This Dover edition, first published in 1997, is an unabridged republication of the music from *Manuel de Falla / El Sombrero de Tres Picos / Le Tricorne / The Three-Cornered Hat / Ballet by Martínez Sierra After a Story by Alarcón*, originally published by J. & W. Chester, Ltd., London, 1921.

The Dover edition adds: a new synopsis, replacing the original detailed one keyed to the numbers in the ballet's piano (rehearsal) score; lists of credits and characters, contents and instrumentation; and an English translation of the footnote, p. 254. The heading on p. 99 has been changed from "The Neighbour's Dance" to "Dance of the Neighbors."

*International Standard Book Number: 0-486-29647-4*

Manufactured in the United States of America
Dover Publications, Inc., 31 East 2nd Street, Mineola, N.Y. 11501

# The Three-Cornered Hat

## Ballet

## Music by Manuel de Falla

∞

The ballet *El sombrero de tres picos* originated as a pantomime based on a short novel of the same name (1874) by Pedro Antonio de Alarcón, itself inspired by a popular *canción*. As *El corregidor y la molinera* (The governor and the miller's wife), the pantomime—with incidental music by de Falla—was first performed in 1917, in Madrid. The stage piece attracted the attention of Sergey Diaghilev, impresario of the Ballets Russes, who persuaded de Falla to rework the music as a ballet.

Ernest Ansermet conducted the premiere of the revised work at London's Alhambra Theatre, 22 July 1919. The story adaptation was by Martínez Sierra. Designs were by Pablo Picasso. Léonide Massine created the role of The Miller, and Tamara Karsavina that of The Miller's Wife.

∞

## Characters

The miller
The miller's wife
The governor (*Corregidor*)
The governor's wife
A dandy
The governor's bodyguard (*Alguacils*)

A mill girl, neighbors, townspeople

*Setting: a rustic mill in the Spanish countryside*

v

# Contents

# Synopsis

## INTRODUCTION

*"Young bride,"* (it is sung) *"lock the door with a crossbar.*
*For, even if the devil is sleeping, like as not he'll wake up!"*

## PART ONE
### Afternoon

Near the mill that also serves as their home, a miller and his lovely young wife take pleasure in a light-hearted afternoon, tending the grapes, playing with a caged blackbird [p. 7], drawing water from the well for their garden [p. 15] and playfully enjoying each other's company. The wife flirts with a passing dandy [p. 16], but her husband sees only his own good fortune to have married such a jewel.

The elderly governor (*Corregidor*) approaches, attended by his wife and retinue [p. 18]. He is taken with the beauty of the miller's wife but, seeing his own wife's suspicious look, continues on his way. The miller's passing flirtation with a girl from the mill angers his wife to tears, yet his earnest vows of love win her over and all is well once again.

At the unexpected return of the philandering governor (this time accompanied only by one bodyguard), the miller quickly hides as his wife pretends to be absorbed in a vivacious solo dance ["Dance of the Miller's Wife (Fandango)," p. 34]. Fooled by her play-acting [p. 62]—which includes a seductive dance with bunches of grapes [p. 63]—the old gallant's clumsy lunge for a kiss ends with his awkward fall to the ground. The miller instantly leaps out of hiding, armed with a stick, pretending to think that robbers have come to ransack his mill. The couple feign sympathy for the old fool, who quickly becomes aware of their game. Furious at being tricked, he leaves to their amusement. The governor's bodyguard appears with a menacing look. His quick departure, however, signals the resumption of the couple's joy and the completion of the fandango.

## PART TWO
### Night

It is evening of the same day—the celebration of St. John's Night. Inside the mill the neighbors celebrate the feast with drink, dance and high spirits ["Dance of the Neighbors (Seguidillas)," p. 99]. The miller dances for his friends ["The Miller's Dance (Farruca)," p. 122]. Festivities are cut short by the arrival of the governor's bodyguards [p. 141], who have come to arrest the miller! Off they go with him, much to the dismay of his wife, who futilely tries to follow. The intimidated partygoers leave one by one. Alone in her grief, the miller's wife withdraws into the silence of her bedroom in the deserted mill [p. 151]. Now, from afar, she hears a song [p. 152] that wounds her aching heart:

*"At night the cuckoo calls, warning married*
*people to shut their bolts tightly, because the*
*devil isn't sleeping! At night the cuckoo calls:*
*'Cuckoo! Cuckoo! Cuckoo!'"*

The cuckoo clock strikes nine [p. 155] as she draws the curtains and extinguishes her light.

With the way cleared for his amorous adventure, the governor appears out of the darkness [p. 157], indulging in the mannerisms of an aging Don Juan ["Dance of the Corregidor," p. 158]. As he crosses a little bridge to the mill, the unexpected darkness of a hidden moon alarms him and he tumbles into the water [p. 165]. His shouts bring the astonished miller's wife to the scene. She is indignant at his intrusion, yet even more furious that this would-be lover persists in his romantic entreaties [p. 167]. Enraged at her rejection, he draws his pistols, but the unintimidated young woman produces her own pistol, intent on shooting the old fool. Suddenly frightened by her target's fearful trembling, the miller's wife runs off. She drops her gun to the ground.

Alone, soaked and shaking with fear and chill, the governor undresses, hangs his clothes and three-cornered hat on a chair to dry, jumps into the miller's bed and draws the curtains.

The escaped miller suddenly reappears [p. 184], unaware of all that has passed. He sees the strange clothes hung next to his bed, draws his own conclusions, picks up the gun and furiously contemplates the darkened bedroom! Torn between doubt and despair, the pacing miller collides in the dark with the laden chair; the governor's three-cornered hat rolls to the ground. The miller kicks the hat in indignation, then suddenly hatches a plot to avenge his imagined betrayal. He exchanges his clothes for the governor's, leaves a note scrawled on the wall—"Dear Governor: I'm off to avenge myself. Your wife, too, is very handsome"—and strides off.

["Final Dance (Jota)," p. 199]: Ignorant of the miller's arrival and departure, the shivering governor peers out of the bed curtains to discover that his clothes have vanished! Even more alarming is the note on the wall! In a frenzy of despair, he puts on the miller's clothes. But as he leaves the mill, the governor is abruptly seized by his own bodyguards, who have returned to search for the escaped miller.

Suddenly, the miller's wife returns, desperately searching for her husband. There he is! Mistaking the disguised governor for the miller, she leaps on the bodyguard!

Now the neighbors appear, attracted by the uproar.

Now the miller is back—still dressed as the governor—hotly pursued by more bodyguards [p. 206]. But there's his wife, protecting the governor (he thinks). The jealous miller leaps on his rival. It is a merry free-for-all.

Adding to the general din and confusion, a large crowd of townspeople appears on the scene, buoyed by the endless festivities of St. John's Night.

No fear, however, for all's well that ends well. To the strains of a festive dance, the miller and his wife are finally reconciled. The tottering Don Juan, now revealed in his true identity, is playfully buffeted by the crowd who end up tossing him in a blanket like some pitiable rag doll [p. 248]—enacting the traditional (and fitting!) ritual of St. John's Night.

English narrative by Ronald Herder, based on the original synopsis of 1921.

The two Spanish songs newly translated by Stanley Appelbaum for this edition.

# Instrumentation

3 Flutes [Flauti/o, Fl.]
    *Flutes 1 & 2 double Piccolos 1 & 2* [Piccolo, Picc.]
2 Oboes [Oboi/e, Ob.]
    *Oboe 2 doubles a second English Horn* [Corno Inglese, C. Ingl.]
English Horn [Corno Inglese, C. Ingl.]
2 Clarinets in A, B♭ [Clarinetti, Clar., Cl. (La, Si♭)
2 Bassoons [Fagotti, Fag.]

4 Horns in F [Corni, Cor. (Fa)]
3 Trumpets in C [Tromb(e) (Do); "Tr." *when playing with trombones*]
3 Trombones [Tromboni, Tromb.]
Tuba [Tuba]

Timpani [Timpani, Timp.]

Percussion:
    Castanets [Castag(nets)]
    Triangle [Triangolo, Triang.]
    Cymbals [Piatti/o]
    Tam-tam [Tam-Tam]
    Xylophone [Xilofono, Xilo(ph).]
    Glockenspiel [Glock.]
    Tubular Bells [Campanelli, Camp.]
    Snare Drum [Tamburo, Tamb.]
    Bass Drum [Cassa]

Mezzo-soprano solo [Mezzo Sop., Canto]
Voices (all) [Voix (toutes)]
Handclappers [Mains frappées]

Piano [Piano, P.]
Celesta [Celesta, C.]
Harp [Arpa, A.]

Violins 1, 2 [Violini, Vl.]
Violas [Viole]
Cellos [Violoncelli, V. Celli, V.C.]
Basses [Contrabassi, C.B.]

# The
# Three-Cornered Hat

## in Full Score

# INTRODUCTION

2

PART ONE
# AFTERNOON

(CURTAIN)

8

Come prima

(sempre Piccolo)

(The Dandy)
⑧ Allegramente (♩ = 126)

*(The Procession)*

Pochissimo più mosso

# DANCE OF THE MILLER'S WIFE (FANDANGO)

In all the bars marked ✳ the last two quavers must be very slightly held back.

50

THE CORREGIDOR

THE MILLER'S WIFE

THE GRAPES

70

Oboe
Clar. 1° Sib
Fag.
2 Cor. in Fa
Timp.
Arpa
Vl. 1°
Vl. 2°
Viole
V. Celli
C.B.
mf
f cresc.
(La♭)
pp
p
sempre 1ª metá
unis. arco
p stacc.

98

## PART TWO
# DANCE OF THE NEIGHBORS (SEGUIDILLAS)

# THE MILLER'S DANCE (FARRUCA)

136

Il doppio più mosso

154

160

*(The Corregidor and the Miller's Wife)*

168

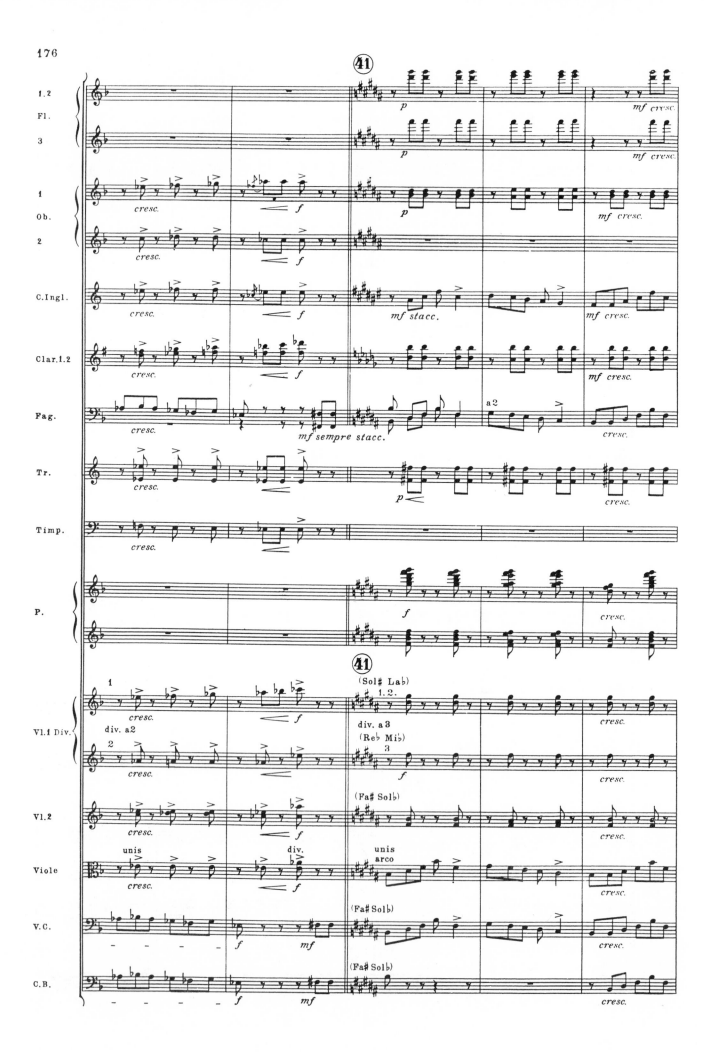

188

190

# FINAL DANCE (JOTA)

*(The tossing of the Corregidor)*

(1.) Dans les representations du Ballet, ce roulement de tambour est substitué par un tutti de Castagnettes sur la scène, pendant la descente du Rideau. La tombée de celui-ci doit, dans ce cas là, coincider avec le dernier accord.

[In ballet performances, this drum roll is replaced by an ensemble of castanets on stage, playing as the curtain descends. In this case, the curtain touch-down should coincide with the last chord.]

END OF EDITION

# Dover Orchestral Scores

**THE SIX BRANDENBURG CONCERTOS AND THE FOUR ORCHESTRAL SUITES IN FULL SCORE, Johann Sebastian Bach.** Complete standard Bach-Gesellschaft editions in large, clear format. Study score. 273pp. 9 × 12. 23376-6 Pa. $11.95

**COMPLETE CONCERTI FOR SOLO KEYBOARD AND ORCHESTRA IN FULL SCORE, Johann Sebastian Bach.** Bach's seven complete concerti for solo keyboard and orchestra in full score from the authoritative Bach-Gesellschaft edition. 206pp. 9 × 12. 24929-8 Pa. $10.95

**THE THREE VIOLIN CONCERTI IN FULL SCORE, Johann Sebastian Bach.** Concerto in A Minor, BWV 1041; Concerto in E Major, BWV 1042; and Concerto for Two Violins in D Minor, BWV 1043. Bach-Gesellschaft edition. 64pp. 9⅜ × 12¼. 25124-1 Pa. $5.95

**GREAT ORGAN CONCERTI, OPP. 4 & 7, IN FULL SCORE, George Frideric Handel.** 12 organ concerti composed by great Baroque master are reproduced in full score from the *Deutsche Handelgesellschaft* edition. 138pp. 9⅜ × 12¼. 24462-8 Pa. $8.95

**COMPLETE CONCERTI GROSSI IN FULL SCORE, George Frideric Handel.** Monumental Opus 6 Concerti Grossi, Opus 3 and "Alexander's Feast" Concerti Grossi—19 in all—reproduced from most authoritative edition. 258pp. 9⅜ × 12¼. 24187-4 Pa. $12.95

**COMPLETE CONCERTI GROSSI IN FULL SCORE, Arcangelo Corelli.** All 12 concerti in the famous late nineteenth-century edition prepared by violinist Joseph Joachim and musicologist Friedrich Chrysander. 240pp. 8⅜ × 11¼. 25606-5 Pa. $12.95

**WATER MUSIC AND MUSIC FOR THE ROYAL FIREWORKS IN FULL SCORE, George Frideric Handel.** Full scores of two of the most popular Baroque orchestral works performed today—reprinted from definitive Deutsche Handelgesellschaft edition. Total of 96pp. 8⅜ × 11. 25070-9 Pa. $6.95

**LATER SYMPHONIES, Wolfgang A. Mozart.** Full orchestral scores to last symphonies (Nos. 35–41) reproduced from definitive Breitkopf & Härtel Complete Works edition. Study score. 285pp. 9 × 12. 23052-X Pa. $11.95

**17 DIVERTIMENTI FOR VARIOUS INSTRUMENTS, Wolfgang A. Mozart.** Sparkling pieces of great vitality and brilliance from 1771-1779; consecutively numbered from 1 to 17. Reproduced from definitive Breitkopf & Härtel Complete Works edition. Study score. 241pp. 9⅜ × 12¼. 23862-8 Pa. $11.95

**PIANO CONCERTOS NOS. 11-16 IN FULL SCORE, Wolfgang Amadeus Mozart.** Authoritative Breitkopf & Härtel edition of six staples of the concerto repertoire, including Mozart's cadenzas for Nos. 12-16. 256pp. 9⅜ × 12¼. 25468-2 Pa. $12.95

**PIANO CONCERTOS NOS. 17-22, Wolfgang Amadeus Mozart.** Six complete piano concertos in full score, with Mozart's own cadenzas for Nos. 17-19. Breitkopf & Härtel edition. Study score. 370pp. 9⅜ × 12¼. 23599-8 Pa. $14.95

**PIANO CONCERTOS NOS. 23-27, Wolfgang Amadeus Mozart.** Mozart's last five piano concertos in full score, plus cadenzas for Nos. 23 and 27, and the Concert Rondo in D Major, K.382. Breitkopf & Härtel edition. Study score. 310pp. 9⅜ × 12¼. 23600-5 Pa. $12.95

**CONCERTI FOR WIND INSTRUMENTS IN FULL SCORE, Wolfgang Amadeus Mozart.** Exceptional volume contains ten pieces for orchestra and wind instruments and includes some of Mozart's finest, most popular music. 272pp. 9⅜ × 12¼. 25228-0 Pa. $13.95

**THE VIOLIN CONCERTI AND THE SINFONIA CONCERTANTE, K.364, IN FULL SCORE, Wolfgang Amadeus Mozart.** All five violin concerti and famed double concerto reproduced from authoritative Breitkopf & Härtel Complete Works Edition. 208pp. 9⅜ × 12½. 25169-1 Pa. $11.95

**SYMPHONIES 88-92 IN FULL SCORE: The Haydn Society Edition, Joseph Haydn.** Full score of symphonies Nos. 88 through 92. Large, readable noteheads, ample margins for fingerings, etc., and extensive Editor's Commentary. 304pp. 9 × 12. (Available in U.S. only) 24445-8 Pa. $13.95

**COMPLETE LONDON SYMPHONIES IN FULL SCORE, Series I and Series II, Joseph Haydn.** Reproduced from the Eulenburg editions are Symphonies Nos. 93–98 (Series I) and Nos. 99–104 (Series II). 800pp. 8⅜ × 11¼. (Available in U.S. only) Series I 24982-4 Pa. $15.95 Series II 24983-2 Pa. $16.95

**FOUR SYMPHONIES IN FULL SCORE, Franz Schubert.** Schubert's four most popular symphonies: No. 4 in C Minor ("Tragic"); No. 5 in B-flat Major; No. 8 in B Minor ("Unfinished"); and No. 9 in C Major ("Great"). Breitkopf & Härtel edition. Study score. 261pp. 9⅜ × 12¼. 23681-1 Pa. $12.95

**GREAT OVERTURES IN FULL SCORE, Carl Maria von Weber.** Overtures to *Oberon, Der Freischutz, Euryanthe* and *Preciosa* reprinted from authoritative Breitkopf & Härtel editions. 112pp. 9 × 12. 25225-6 Pa. $8.95

**SYMPHONIES NOS. 1, 2, 3, AND 4 IN FULL SCORE, Ludwig van Beethoven.** Republication of H. Litolff edition. 272pp. 9 × 12. 26033-X Pa. $10.95

**SYMPHONIES NOS. 5, 6 AND 7 IN FULL SCORE, Ludwig van Beethoven.** Republication of the H. Litolff edition. 272pp. 9 × 12. 26034-8 Pa. $10.95

**SYMPHONIES NOS. 8 AND 9 IN FULL SCORE, Ludwig van Beethoven.** Republication of the H. Litolff edition. 256pp. 9 × 12. 26035-6 Pa. $10.95

**SIX GREAT OVERTURES IN FULL SCORE, Ludwig van Beethoven.** Six staples of the orchestral repertoire from authoritative Breitkopf & Härtel edition. *Leonore Overtures*, Nos. 1-3; Overtures to *Coriolanus, Egmont, Fidelio.* 288pp. 9 × 12. 24789-9 Pa. $13.95

**COMPLETE PIANO CONCERTOS IN FULL SCORE, Ludwig van Beethoven.** Complete scores of five great Beethoven piano concertos, with all cadenzas as he wrote them, reproduced from authoritative Breitkopf & Härtel edition. New table of contents. 384pp. 9⅜ × 12¼. 24563-2 Pa. $14.95

**GREAT ROMANTIC VIOLIN CONCERTI IN FULL SCORE, Ludwig van Beethoven, Felix Mendelssohn and Peter Ilyitch Tchaikovsky.** The Beethoven Op. 61, Mendelssohn, Op. 64 and Tchaikovsky, Op. 35 concertos reprinted from the Breitkopf & Härtel editions. 224pp. 9 × 12. 24989-1 Pa. $10.95

**MAJOR ORCHESTRAL WORKS IN FULL SCORE, Felix Mendelssohn.** Generally considered to be Mendelssohn's finest orchestral works, here in one volume are: the complete *Midsummer Night's Dream; Hebrides Overture; Calm Sea and Prosperous Voyage Overture;* Symphony No. 3 in A ("Scottish"); and Symphony No. 4 in A ("Italian"). Breitkopf & Härtel edition. Study score. 406pp. 9 × 12. 23184-4 Pa. $16.95

**COMPLETE SYMPHONIES, Johannes Brahms.** Full orchestral scores. No. 1 in C Minor, Op. 68; No. 2 in D Major, Op. 73; No. 3 in F Major, Op. 90; and No. 4 in E Minor, Op. 98. Reproduced from definitive Vienna Gesellschaft der Musikfreunde edition. Study score. 344pp. 9 × 12. 23053-8 Pa. $13.95

*Available from your music dealer or write for free Music Catalog to*
*Dover Publications, Inc., Dept. MUBI, 31 East 2nd Street, Mineola, N.Y. 11501.*

## *Dover Orchestral Scores*

**THREE ORCHESTRAL WORKS IN FULL SCORE: Academic Festival Overture, Tragic Overture and Variations on a Theme by Joseph Haydn, Johannes Brahms.** Reproduced from the authoritative Breitkopf & Härtel edition three of Brahms's great orchestral favorites. Editor's commentary in German and English. 112pp. 9⅜ × 12¼. 24637-X Pa. **$8.95**

**COMPLETE CONCERTI IN FULL SCORE, Johannes Brahms.** Piano Concertos Nos. 1 and 2; Violin Concerto, Op. 77; Concerto for Violin and Cello, Op. 102. Definitive Breitkopf & Härtel edition. 352pp. 9⅜ × 12¼. 24170-X Pa. **$15.95**

**COMPLETE SYMPHONIES IN FULL SCORE, Robert Schumann.** No. 1 in B-flat Major, Op. 38 ("Spring"); No. 2 in C Major, Op. 61; No. 3 in E Flat Major, Op. 97 ("Rhenish"); and No. 4 in D Minor, Op. 120. Breitkopf & Härtel editions. Study score. 416pp. 9⅜ × 12¼. 24013-4 Pa. **$17.95**

**GREAT WORKS FOR PIANO AND ORCHESTRA IN FULL SCORE, Robert Schumann.** Collection of three superb pieces for piano and orchestra, including the popular Piano Concerto in A Minor. Breitkopf & Härtel edition. 183pp. 9⅜ × 12¼. 24340-0 Pa. **$10.95**

**THE PIANO CONCERTOS IN FULL SCORE, Frédéric Chopin.** The authoritative Breitkopf & Härtel full-score edition in one volume of Piano Concertos No. 1 in E Minor and No. 2 in F Minor. 176pp. 9 × 12. 25835-1 Pa. **$9.95**

**THE PIANO CONCERTI IN FULL SCORE, Franz Liszt.** Available in one volume the Piano Concerto No. 1 in E-flat Major and the Piano Concerto No. 2 in A Major—are among the most studied, recorded and performed of all works for piano and orchestra. 144pp. 9 × 12. 25221-3 Pa. **$8.95**

**SYMPHONY NO. 8 IN G MAJOR, OP. 88, SYMPHONY NO. 9 IN E MINOR, OP. 95 ("NEW WORLD") IN FULL SCORE, Antonín Dvořák.** Two celebrated symphonies by the great Czech composer, the Eighth and the immensely popular Ninth, "From the New World" in one volume. 272pp. 9 × 12. 24749-X Pa. **$12.95**

**FOUR ORCHESTRAL WORKS IN FULL SCORE: Rapsodie Espagnole, Mother Goose Suite, Valses Nobles et Sentimentales, and Pavane for a Dead Princess, Maurice Ravel.** Four of Ravel's most popular orchestral works, reprinted from original full-score French editions. 240pp. 9⅜ × 12¼. (Not available in France or Germany) 25962-5 Pa. **$12.95**

**DAPHNIS AND CHLOE IN FULL SCORE, Maurice Ravel.** Definitive full-score edition of Ravel's rich musical setting of a Greek fable by Longus is reprinted here from the original French edition. 320pp. 9⅜ × 12¼. (Not available in France or Germany) 25826-2 Pa. **$14.95**

**THREE GREAT ORCHESTRAL WORKS IN FULL SCORE, Claude Debussy.** Three favorites by influential modernist: *Prélude à l'Après-midi d'un Faune, Nocturnes,* and *La Mer.* Reprinted from early French editions. 279pp. 9 × 12. 24441-5 Pa. **$12.95**

**SYMPHONY IN D MINOR IN FULL SCORE, César Franck.** Superb, authoritative edition of Franck's only symphony, an often-performed and recorded masterwork of late French romantic style. 160pp. 9 × 12. 25373-2 Pa. **$9.95**

**THE GREAT WALTZES IN FULL SCORE, Johann Strauss, Jr.** Complete scores of eight melodic masterpieces: The Beautiful Blue Danube, Emperor Waltz, Tales of the Vienna Woods, Wiener Blut, four more. Authoritative editions. 336pp. 8⅞ × 11¼. 26009-7 Pa. **$13.95**

**FOURTH, FIFTH AND SIXTH SYMPHONIES IN FULL SCORE, Peter Ilyitch Tchaikovsky.** Complete orchestral scores of Symphony No. 4 in F minor, Op. 36; Symphony No. 5 in E minor, Op. 64; Symphony No. 6 in B minor, "Pathetique," Op. 74. Study score. Breitkopf & Härtel editions. 480pp. 9⅜ × 12¼. 23861-X Pa. **$19.95**

**ROMEO AND JULIET OVERTURE AND CAPRICCIO ITALIEN IN FULL SCORE, Peter Ilyitch Tchaikovsky.** Two of Russian master's most popular compositions in high quality, inexpensive reproduction. From authoritative Russian edition. 208pp. 8⅝ × 11½. 25217-5 Pa. **$9.95**

**NUTCRACKER SUITE IN FULL SCORE, Peter Ilyitch Tchaikovsky.** Among the most popular ballet pieces ever created—a complete, inexpensive, high-quality score to study and enjoy. 128pp. 9 × 12. 25379-1 Pa. **$8.95**

**TONE POEMS, SERIES I: DON JUAN, TOD UND VERKLARUNG, and DON QUIXOTE, Richard Strauss.** Three of the most often performed and recorded works in entire orchestral repertoire, reproduced in full score from original editions. Study score. 286pp. 9⅜ × 12¼. (Available in U.S. only) 23754-0 Pa. **$13.95**

**TONE POEMS, SERIES II: TILL EULENSPIEGELS LUSTIGE STREICHE, ALSO SPRACH ZARATHUSTRA, and EIN HELDENLEBEN, Richard Strauss.** Three important orchestral works, including very popular *Till Eulenspiegel's Merry Pranks,* reproduced in full score from original editions. Study score. 315pp. 9⅜ × 12¼. (Available in U.S. only) 23755-9 Pa. **$14.95**

**DAS LIED VON DER ERDE IN FULL SCORE, Gustav Mahler.** Mahler's masterpiece, a fusion of song and symphony, reprinted from the original 1912 Universal Edition. English translations of song texts. 160pp. 9 × 12. 25657-X Pa. **$8.95**

**SYMPHONIES NOS. 1 AND 2 IN FULL SCORE, Gustav Mahler.** Unabridged, authoritative Austrian editions of Symphony No. 1 in D Major ("Titan") and Symphony No. 2 in C Minor ("Resurrection"). 384pp. 8⅛ × 11. 25473-9 Pa. **$14.95**

**SYMPHONIES NOS. 3 AND 4 IN FULL SCORE, Gustav Mahler.** Two brilliantly contrasting masterworks—one scored for a massive ensemble, the other for small orchestra and soloist—reprinted from authoritative Viennese editions. 368pp. 9⅜ × 12¼. 26166-2 Pa. **$15.95**

**SYMPHONY NO. 8 IN FULL SCORE, Gustav Mahler.** Superb authoritative edition of massive, complex "Symphony of a Thousand." Scored for orchestra, eight solo voices, double chorus, boys' choir and organ. Reprint of Izdatel'stvo "Muzyka," Moscow, edition. Translation of texts. 272pp. 9⅜ × 12¼. 26022-4 Pa. **$12.95**

**THE FIREBIRD IN FULL SCORE (Original 1910 Version), Igor Stravinsky.** Handsome, inexpensive edition of modern masterpiece, renowned for brilliant orchestration, glowing color. Authoritative Russian edition. 176pp. 9⅜ × 12¼. (Available in U.S. only) 25535-2 Pa. **$10.95**

**PETRUSHKA IN FULL SCORE: Original Version, Igor Stravinsky.** The definitive full-score edition of Stravinsky's masterful score for the great Ballets Russes 1911 production of *Petrushka.* 160pp. 9⅜ × 12¼. (Available in U.S. only) 25680-4 Pa. **$9.95**

**THE RITE OF SPRING IN FULL SCORE, Igor Stravinsky.** A reprint of the original full-score edition of the most famous musical work of the 20th century, created as a ballet score for Diaghilev's Ballets Russes. 176pp. 9⅜ × 12¼. (Available in U.S. only) 25857-2 Pa. **$9.95**

*Available from your music dealer or write for* **free** *Music Catalog to Dover Publications, Inc., Dept. MUBI, 31 East 2nd Street, Mineola, N.Y. 11501.*